For Mark and Scott Lowrey

with love.

Six Silver Spoons

by Janette Sebring Lowrey

Pictures by Robert Quackenbush

An I CAN READ History Book

Harper & Row, Publishers

New York   Evanston   San Francisco   London

Library of Congress Catalog Card Number: 77-105469
Standard Book Number 06-024036-9 (Trade)
Standard Book Number 06-024037-7 (Harpercrest)

FIRST EDITION

CONTENTS

CHAPTER ONE

Time To Go

"Debby! Debby! Wake up!"

Tim called from the bottom

of the stairs.

The sun was not up yet.

"Wake up, Debby! Wake up!"

Tim called again.

"It is almost time to go!"

Debby hopped out of bed

and ran to the door.

"I'm up, Tim!" Debby called down.

Today she and Father and Tim

were going to Grandmother's farm.

It was fifteen miles away—

near Lexington.

Grandmother had not been well.

She had sent for Mother ten days ago.

But now Grandmother was well again.

Mother was coming home.

Tomorrow was Mother's birthday.

They had a surprise for her—

six beautiful silver spoons

made by Paul Revere.

Father said Mr. Revere was
the finest silversmith in Boston.
Debby picked up Miss Arabella Doll
and ran downstairs.
Hannah was in the kitchen.

"Eat your breakfast," she said.

"Is Father here?" Debby asked.

"He had to go to Watertown,"
Hannah said.

"Looks like we are going to have
more trouble with the British."

"But Watertown is miles away!"
cried Debby.

"He can't get back in time
to take us to Grandmother's!"

"Fiddlesticks!" said Hannah.

"It's not so far.

He left hours ago!"

The front door slammed.

"There's Father now!" said Debby.

But it was not Father. It was Tim.

"I took Dobbin and the shay

around to the front," Tim said.

"We are ready to go."

"Debby is scared your Pa

won't get back," Hannah told him.

"He will come if he can," said Tim.

"I hear that the British are ready

to march to Concord," said Hannah.

"To take the guns

we have stored there," Tim added.

"Will they march today?" Debby asked.
"Oh, Hannah! Will they let us
go to the farm for Mother?"
"No telling," Hannah said.

Ten o'clock, eleven o'clock,

twelve o'clock . . .

Still Father had not come!

At two o'clock, Tim decided

to go and get the spoons

from Paul Revere's shop.

"It will save time," he said.

"Father will surely be here

by the time I get back."

"I am going with you," said Debby.

Soft white clouds

sailed in the April sky.

Apple trees were in bloom.

But there were soldiers

in North Square.

"British soldiers," Debby said.

"Redcoats," said Tim.

"Father says they should go
back to England."

They hurried across the busy square
and down to Clark's Wharf.

There stood the shop with its sign:

PAUL REVERE, SILVERSMITH

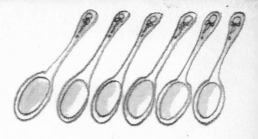

CHAPTER TWO

Redcoats in the Square

Paul Revere was not in his shop.

"Your spoons are ready,"

said the clerk.

He gave Tim

a little roll of soft gray flannel.

"Open it," he said. "Look at them."

Tim untied the bundle.

He spread it out on the counter.

"How beautiful!" Debby exclaimed.

"Oh, Tim! I wish we could show them

to Mother this minute!"

The clock on the wall struck three.

Tim tied up the spoons again.

"We should have been on the road

hours ago," he said.

"Come on, Debby."

A company of Redcoats

marched into North Square.

They were on their way

to Boston Common.

"The British are up to something,"
Tim said.

"They may not let us go now.
We should have left at daybreak."

"Without Father?" Debby asked.

"We could go by ourselves
if we had to," Tim said.

At the corner, they began to run.

They raced down the street.

Hannah met them at the door.

"Your Pa's not here yet," she said.

"Then he is not coming," said Tim.

"We will go by ourselves.

Come on, Debby."

"What will your Pa say?" cried Hannah.

"Land sakes! Aren't you afraid?"

She hurried after them

with a basket of food and Miss Arabella.

"We will be just fine, Hannah,"

Debby said.

Tim gave Dobbin a little slap

with the reins,

and they were on their way

to the Town Gates.

On Debby's lap lay the silver spoons.

In her arms she held Miss Arabella.

Two Redcoats stood at the Town Gates.

One of them came up to the shay.

"Two youngsters alone!" he exclaimed.

"And where might you be going?"

"To Grandmother's farm,

near Lexington," Tim answered.

"What have you there, little girl?"

the soldier asked.

"My doll," said Debby,

"and a present for my mother."

"Let me see that," said the soldier.

"Aha!" he said.

"Six handsome silver spoons!

These are worth money.

We will keep them."

Debby began to cry.

Tim jumped out of the shay.

He was very angry.

"Give the spoons to my sister!"
he cried.

"They are a present for my mother!"
The Redcoats laughed.

"Get back in the shay, young sir,"
one of them said.

"You will be lucky if we let *you* go."

CHAPTER THREE

The Captain and the Doll

A Redcoat came riding

down Lexington Road.

"Here comes the captain,"

said one of the soldiers.

"He will send you back to Boston."

"Don't cry, Debby," Tim said.

But Debby could not stop.

Mother's birthday present was gone!

The captain got off his horse.

He came over to Tim.

"Why is the little girl crying?"

he asked.

Tim told him about the spoons.

"Are you taking them to your mother?"

the captain asked.

"Yes, sir," said Tim.

"Give me the spoons,"

the captain said to the soldier.

"Give me your doll's dress and bonnet,

little girl."

He rolled the spoons up tight

in their flannel wrapper.

Over this

he slipped Miss Arabella's dress.

On the end of the roll

he tied the doll's bonnet.

"Now," he said to Debby, "you have two dolls. Do not tell anyone that you have a present for your mother."

"Thank you ever so much,"
said Debby.

"I have a little girl,"
the captain said, "in faraway England. She is just about your age.

You must be on your way now,"
he said to Tim.

"Take care of your little sister."

"I will," Tim promised.

"Good-bye!" said Debby.

In one arm she cuddled Miss Arabella.

In the other she held

the make-believe doll.

"Miss Arabella is going the rest of

the way in her petticoat," said Debby.

"But she doesn't mind."

Tim gave Dobbin a flick of the whip.

The shay rolled through

the Town Gates.

They were on the road at last.

CHAPTER FOUR

The British Are Coming!

It was night

when they got to the farm.

Tim drove into the barnyard.

Mother and Grandmother heard them.

They came running out to meet them.

"Bless my soul!" cried Grandmother.

"Tim! Debby!" Mother said.

"How glad I am to see you!"

The night wind was cold.

But the farmhouse kitchen

was warm and bright.

"But what is this?" said Grandmother.

"Miss Arabella in her petticoat?"

Quickly, Debby hid the

make-believe doll in her coat pocket.

Mother must not see the silver spoons

until tomorrow.

Grandmother took Miss Arabella

from Debby.

"We will make her a new dress,"

she said.

"But where is Father?" asked Mother.

"Did he send you children alone?"

"He had to go to Watertown

last night," Tim said.

"We waited and waited.

And then we came by ourselves."

"Tomorrow is your birthday,"

said Debby.

"So it is," said Mother, smiling.

Tim and Debby put their coats down

on the settee.

"The spoons are in my pocket,"

Debby whispered.

A horse clattered into the barnyard.

"It's Father!" Debby cried.

Before anyone could get to the door,

Father was in the kitchen.

Everyone was talking at once.

"Let Father talk," said Mother.

Father told them that the British

were coming for the guns

stored in Concord.

"We believe," he said, "that they

will march tonight.

But when they get to Concord,

they will find nothing there.

We have moved the guns out.

We have stored them

in new hiding places

in other villages.

We have worked very hard."

Grandmother was frightened.

"Then they will come up

Lexington Road!" she said.

"Quick! Put on your coats, children!

Help me get some food and my knives

and forks and the silver bowls.

We will go down to the shed

at the back of the orchard.

We are too near the road here!"

"There is no hurry," Father said.

"They will not start out

before the moon rises.

And we may have news before that."

They put out all the candles.

Debby sat by the front window.

She listened for

the tramp of marching feet.

Tim and Father

were out at the edge of the road.

They were watching and listening too.

CHAPTER FIVE

Mother's Surprise

The moon came up.

Fields turned silver

in the silver light.

After a while, Debby put

her head down on her arms

and went to sleep.

The clatter of hoofs woke her.

She could hear someone's voice.

She ran out to the steps.

A horseman slowed down

and shouted to Father.

"The British have left Boston!

The Redcoats are coming!"

In an instant he was gone.

He galloped away toward Lexington.

Tim and Father ran back to the house.

"That was Paul Revere!"

said Father.

"Paul Revere!" Debby said.

She thought of the silver spoons.

She ran back to the kitchen

and picked up her coat.

She put her hand in the pocket.

The make-believe doll was gone.

"I know I put it there," she said.

She looked under the settee.

It was not there.

It was not on the table.

It was not on any of the chairs.

Tim was with Father.

They were taking Grandmother's things

to the shed in the orchard.

Everyone was busy.

Debby began to cry.

"I've lost them!"

"What is the matter?" Mother asked.

"I've lost your birthday present!"

Debby sobbed.

Father and Tim came in.

"I've lost the spoons!" she said.

"No, you have not," Tim said.

He took the make-believe doll

from his pocket.

"Here they are, Debby. I thought

they would be safer with me."

"Let's give them to Mother now,"

said Father.

"It is one o'clock of a brand new day.

It is Mother's birthday."

Mother untied the little bundle

and saw the six silver spoons.

"Oh!" she said.

"Such beautiful spoons!"

"Paul Revere made them,"

Tim told her proudly.

Clang! Clang! Clang!

"That is the Lexington

meetinghouse bell," said Father.

"It is the call to arms.

I must go to Concord

to meet the Redcoats.

Tim will take you

down to the orchard.

Stay there

till the troops have gone past.

You will be safe."

"Yes," said Debby,

"and so will the silver spoons!"

AUTHOR'S NOTE

Two hundred years ago our country was a group of thirteen British colonies. The King and Parliament of England made our laws and set the taxes. Governors and soldiers were sent over from England to see that these laws were obeyed. The colonists believed that they should make their own laws. They had to fight for the right to do so. They gathered large stores of guns and ammunition and hid them from the British.

One of the towns where these supplies were hidden was Concord, Massachusetts, not far from Boston. The British found out about it and decided to take or destroy the supplies. But the colonists were watching. On the late afternoon of April 18, 1775, British troops marched across Boston to the Charles River, where boats were waiting for them. Everyone in Boston knew that the Redcoats would be on their way to Concord that night.

Paul Revere crossed by boat to Charlestown, and rode fast, stopping at every farmhouse to give warning that the British were coming. He brought the news to Lexington around midnight. The meetinghouse bell rang out the alarm. Soon bells in all the neighboring towns were ringing, drums were beating, and men were hurrying to Concord. Early in the morning when the British got to Concord, five hundred Minutemen were ready for them. They drove the British back toward Lexington and Boston.

The battle at Concord was the first battle of the American Revolution.